Myth Quest

Airavata

ELEPHANT OF THE CLOUDS

retold by Anu Kumar

illustrations by Maya Magical Studios

First published in 2011 by Hachette India
(Registered name: Hachette Book Publishing India Pvt. Ltd)
An Hachette UK company
www.hachetteindia.com

SRD

ISBN 978-93-5009-298-9

Hachette Book Publishing India Pvt. Ltd
612/614 (6th Floor), Time Tower,
M.G. Road, Sector 28, Gurgaon 122001, India

Typeset in Adobe Garamond Pro 13/16
by Eleven Arts, New Delhi

Printed and bound in India by
Manipal Technologies Limited, Manipal

Welcome to the world of MythQuest

Discover the fables and legends about the origin, history, deities, ancestors and heroes of India.

While the term 'myth' in common conversation means a false story, in the world of religion, folklore and magic, myths are considered 'true'. They tell stories of the creation of the universe, the eternal battle between good and evil, and the history of humankind itself.

The main characters in our myths are bigger and better than any modern superheroes. They are birds and beasts, gods and demons, kings and queens, generals and warriors, sages and gurus, each with extraordinary powers that changed the course of history and the fate of the human race.

The people to whom a myth belongs consider it a true account of their past millions of years ago. Even today, they continue to worship the gods and goddesses, follow the rituals and read the texts that developed from these myths.

Hachette India's MythQuest series brings to you fascinating stories from the vast treasures of ancient mythology. Read them all—and become a MythMaster!

Mythological characters and events have been described in different ways in different versions of ancient texts. We have chosen the most interesting and key stories to build a comprehensive account for the young reader.

This story is about . . .

. . . Airavata, the divine king of elephants. This magnificent white elephant carried Indra, the Lord of Heaven, across the skies. This sentinel at Heaven's portal is also known as Ardha-Matanga—elephant of the clouds, Naga-malla—the fighting elephant and Arkasodara—brother of the Sun.

Airavata was huge and immensely strong, but despite his size, he was nimble and quick. He guarded the entrance to Heaven, and also fought alongside Indra and carried him into many great battles.

He is mentioned in the Puranic texts, the Ramayana, the Mahabharata and the Matangalila, or The Elephant Lore of the Hindus by Nilakantha.

In Thailand, Airavata is known as Erawan and depicted as a huge elephant with three to thirty-three heads. The heads are often shown with more than two tusks.

White elephants are considered sacred in South Asia, and thought to bring good luck, rain and a bountiful harvest. Airavata or Erawan is present on the national flag of Laos as well as the personal standards of the kings of Thailand.

One of the earlier incarnations of Buddha was Vessantara, a crown prince of the kingdom of Sivi. He owned a magical white elephant that drew rain clouds.

Read Airavata's story, sometimes rainy and wet, and sometimes dark and full of danger . . .

CHAPTER ONE

AN EGGSHELL AND EIGHT ELEPHANTS

Long, long, very long ago, at a time that only memory and retelling has recorded, Lord Brahma, the Creator of the Universe, held in his hands two halves of a giant eggshell. He held these carefully as he chanted the seven sacred hymns of creation.

The universe was already teeming with newly created beings, but it was yet missing a creature that was majestic yet gentle, mighty yet kind, powerful yet wise.

The extraordinary egg that Brahma held belonged to Kadru. She and Vinata were two of sage Kashyapa's many wives. Kadru had wanted many offspring, while Vinata had desired only two, but very powerful ones, mightier than any of Kadru's children.

Each had been granted her wish by the sage. Kadru laid a thousand eggs that hatched into a thousand snakes, and she became the mother of the entire race of serpents. From one of Vinata's eggs hatched Aruna, who became the father of Jatayu, the king of the birds, and the charioteer of the Sun God, Surya.

From the second egg hatched the all-powerful Garuda, who became the vehicle of Lord Vishnu. It was the broken halves of the latter egg that Brahma held in his hands as he chanted.

As Brahma reached the end of his incantations, there emerged from the half of the egg in his right hand, eight majestic bull elephants—and the first one of these was Airavata, an awesome elephant, spotless as a summer cloud, white as winter snow.

The bull elephants were the Dig-gajas, the vehicles of the Dik-palas, the guardian gods who presided over the eight points of the compass—the four cardinal and the four intermediate directions. The gods and the elephants were both known as the Lokpalas, as they were responsible for ensuring that no evil or harm befell the universe.

From the eggshell in Brahma's left hand emerged eight majestic cow elephants, each one to partner one of the bull elephants. The first among the cow

elephants was Abharamu, who went on to become Airavata's wife.

So this is how the universe was secured by the eight sentinels: there was Indra at the east post, at the portal to Heaven, or Svarga, with Airavata and the female elephant, Abharamu; Varuna on the western end, with

Anjana and his cow elephant Anjanavati; Kubera to the north, with Sarvabhauma; Yama at the south gate, with Vamana and Pingala; Agni to the south-east with Pundarika and Kapila; Surya at the south-west with Kumuda and Anupama; Vayu at the north-west frontier with Pushpadanta and Subhadanti; and Soma at the north-east quarter with Supratika and Tamrakarni.

It is also said that Iravati, the daughter of Kadru and sage Kashyapa, was the mother of Airavata. Iravati's divine child grew up to be the foremost of all the elephants.

It is also believed that Airavata was crowned the king of elephants by Prithu, the first king of earth and an avatar of Lord Vishnu himself.

In another story, Airavata is believed to have emerged out of the foaming waters during the *samudra manthan*, or the churning of the Ocean of Milk. After a curse from the sage Durvasa, the gods lost all their strength and their immortality. In an effort to regain their lost powers, the *devas* entered into an alliance with the *asuras* and together they decided to churn the Ocean of Milk, for within its depths were hidden many treasures including the coveted *amrita*, or the nectar of immortality.

In order to churn the ocean, the *devas* and the *asuras* used Mount Mandara as the tool and the great serpent Vasuki as the rope. The gods pulled from one end while the *asuras* held the other. As a result of the terrible churning, the ocean yielded a deadly poison called Halahala. This poison was so dangerous that none of the *devas* or *asuras* could go near it and they all fled in fear of its fumes. Finally, Lord Shiva came forward to help and cupped the poison in his palms and drank it. As a result of this act his throat turned blue and he came to be known as Neelakantha, or the blue-throated one.

Thereafter, the churning continued and gradually precious objects called *ratnas* began to emerge out of the ocean. The fourteen *ratnas* that emerged included Uchchaishravas, the seven-headed flying horse, Kamadhenu, the divine cow, Parijat, the eternally flowering tree, Airavata, the great white elephant of the clouds, and Dhanvantari, the Physician of the Gods, holding the urn of *amrita*.

The moment Indra saw this beautiful white elephant emerge from the foaming waters, he claimed it as his own and thus Airavata became Indra's mount or vehicle. It is said that this is the reason why his name is said to mean 'born of, or produced by water'. He also became associated with water in another way as he could draw clouds and thus create rain.

CHAPTER TWO

FALLING RAIN AND WASTED WINGS

Airavata is closely connected with water. Born of the Ocean of Milk, he was also gifted with the remarkable ability of being able to draw clouds and thus create rain, which in turn, ensured the continuation of life on earth.

Airavata had several tusks and many curling trunks that could create clouds. The mighty elephant would stretch his trunks into lakes, rivers, seas and all water reservoirs, suck up the water and then spray it into the clouds with a big whoosh. Lord Indra would then hurl his thunderbolt—the four-edged Vajra—at dark rain-bearing clouds, forcing them to release rain so that the parched earth would again turn green with grass,

shrubs, plants and trees. At different times he released different kinds of rain—a continuous drizzle, a cooling shower, or a torrential downpour. It was thus that the waters of the earth and Heaven were forever bound together in a rain cycle.

It is said that at the beginning, and no one really knows when the beginning was, all the celestial elephants that had descended from the eight Dig-gajas could sweep up water from the lakes and rivers, and fill the clouds with moisture. This would cause rain that would fall on the earth and make it fertile, so human life could continue.

However, with the passage of time, most elephants lost this magical ability, except the great Airavata.

Besides being able to create rain, Airavata could also fly across the skies and thus he was a perfect vehicle for Indra, who often travelled to the corners of the universe to fight great battles. As the Lord of Heaven and the King of Gods, it was Indra's duty to protect the *devas* and settle disputes between them. He also intervened every time an *asura* or *rakshasa* threatened the order of the universe. And who better to aid him on his many quests, journeys and wars than the mighty Airavata?

In the very early days of the universe, elephants were also the proud owners of wings. Spreading out their mammoth wings, these huge creatures could fly across the vast skies at great speed. However, this power, too, was taken away when one elephant accidentally disturbed a sage.

There was once a sage called Dirghatapas, and like a great many sages, he had been meditating under a tree for decades upon decades. In fact, his name itself meant 'long penance'. While he was immersed in his meditations, an elephant, having flown huge distances across the universe, and quite exhausted due to his travels, finally came to rest on the very branch of the tree under which Dirghatapas sat.

The tree was an old one, and could not take the weight of the elephant. As the huge elephant sat on the branch, its head on its forelegs, the branch staggered under its weight. It cracked nosily and finally gave way, crashing down on top of the sage.

The sage's long and arduous penance was disrupted, and he was enraged. Standing up, he cursed the elephant angrily: 'These wings of yours that you use to fly about so carelessly, will no longer be of any use to you, or to anyone of your kind. From now, you will be bound to earth and will have to carry humans upon your back.' And that was that. The moment the sage uttered the curse, elephants lost the use of their wings and their lovely feathers wilted and fell away.

And even the mighty Airavata was shorn of his wings and could no longer fly across the universe. However, being the most magical and powerful of all the elephants, Airavata could still stride across all the three worlds of Heaven, earth and *patala*, or the underworld, while the other elephants became bound to land.

In keeping with sage's curse, all the descendents of the noble Dig-gajas were forced to carry kings and princes into battle. In later times, some even became poor beasts of burden.

CHAPTER THREE

LITTLE HANUMAN PLAYS WITH AIRAVATA

Airavata's power lay in his position as first among all elephants. After all, he had been made the king of all elephants by Lord Brahma himself.

According to an ancient legend, Brahma crowned Prithu the first king of the earth after the Great Flood had ended.

During this time Brahma also anointed other creatures as kings of their respective species. It was during this time that Airavata was crowned king of elephants by the supreme deity and Creator of the

Universe. He was also a vehicle of the King of Gods, Indra, and thus a demigod himself, worshipped by humans and respected by all. Airavata was also immensely strong. And despite his size, he was a fleet-footed creature, able to outrun any creature smaller than himself. He could cover the universe in just three strides. This great elephant guarded the entrance to Heaven and also accompanied Indra in his wars against all kinds of evil creatures.

However, there was a time when someone did not pay heed to how big, or strong, or important Airavata was! This someone was young Hanuman, the son of Vayu, the powerful Wind God and Anjana, a female *vanara* or monkey. Hanuman was an extraordinary child, restless and curious, and bestowed with unimaginable strength. For instance, once he mistook the Sun for a mango and rushed towards the sky to grab it in his bare hand!

Another time, he saw Rahu, the *asura* with the cut-off immortal head, making his way to the Sun to gobble it up and cause an eclipse. Hanuman mistook him to be a worm, and made his way quickly to swallow him as a snack. Running for his life, Rahu sought refuge with Indra. The King of Gods and Lord of Heaven hefted his deadly thunderbolt, mounted Airavata and marched off to look for the mischief-making Hanuman.

Lightning flashed, ripping the skies, and clouds thundered threateningly as Indra's anger rose. However,

neither the sound of Indra's wrath, nor the sight of him armed to the teeth atop his swaggering mount, frightened Hanuman a teeny-weeny bit. Instead, it only excited him some more.

Coming face to face with Indra atop the divine Airavata, Hanuman simply grinned. He thought the mighty Airavata was a mere toy, and made a grab for him, seizing him by his trunk. Surprised by the young one's aggression, and offended by his insult to Airavata,

Indra struck Hanuman with his thunderbolt. Stunned by its force, Hanuman fell, hurtling down to earth. Luckily, his father Vayu came to his rescue, catching him speedily in midair.

Nobody escaped Vayu's wrath. And the Wind God was very angry when he saw his beloved son injured by Indra. Infuriated, he inhaled such a mighty breath that all the air in the universe was sucked away. Then he cursed loudly: 'Let all those who have harmed Anjana's son choke to death.'

Immediately, there was great pandemonium in the universe. Everyone needed air to survive.

The gods were repentant. They gathered and went to Lord Vayu in a group, to ask for his pardon. Many of them now showered blessings and boons on the Wind God's son, Hanuman.

Brahma proclaimed: 'May you live as long as Brahma himself lives.'

Vishnu said: 'May you live all your life as the greatest devotee of God.'

Indra declared: 'No weapon of any kind will wound or hit your body.'

Agni pronounced: 'Fire will never affect you.'

Kala announced: 'May death never court you.'

And all the *devas* or gods spoke as one: 'None will ever equal you in strength.'

Brahma concluded the session by bestowing on Hanuman a power greater than even Vayu and

Garuda, the vehicle of Lord Vishnu, and blessed him with a speed faster than that of the mightiest wind. However, it was decided that Hanuman himself would stay unaware of his extraordinary powers until a good deed by him would bring his superhuman abilities to light.

Now the father was quieted down and he restored all the air in the universe and everything was as before. Hanuman himself was stunned by the blow and made sure he never offended Airavata again. In fact, after this incident, everyone realized how much Indra loved his elephant and no one dared to pick up a fight with Airavata or insult him in any way.

CHAPTER FOUR

A GARLAND AND A CURSE

As Indra's favoured follower, Airavata was treated with respect and his own gentle nature found him many friends. However, there was one time when the elephant-king managed to offend a sage and incurred the full power of his wrath.

This sage was no other than the powerful Durvasa, who cursed him and the rest of the gods for their bad behaviour. As a result of this terrible curse, Airavata lost his spotless white coat, and the gods, having angered Durvasa, lost their gift of immortality.

It so happened that once the sage Durvasa paid a visit to the gods. He was given a reverent welcome, for the gods lived in awe of Durvasa, as he had acquired immense powers through long years of meditation. The gods were also quite terrified of causing any situation that would make Durvasa lose his cool, as the sage was known for his bad temper.

Indra, the King of Gods, himself received sage Durvasa in person at the gates of Heaven and the *apsaras*, or the celestial nymphs, showered him with rose petals. One of the most beautiful *apsaras*, Menaka, presented him with a garland strung with exquisite *kalpaka* flowers. The garland was so divine that its fragrance soon filled the entire universe.

Sage Durvasa was pleased with the reception he had been accorded—and the garland. However, being an ascetic, he knew that he should not be attached to any object, so he decided to gift it in turn to Indra. The King of Gods was delighted with the garland and couldn't stop inhaling its fragrance.

After a while, the sage prepared to go back to earth. A magnificent farewell ceremony was held in his honour. Durvasa was pleased with the care and attention that had been lavished upon him by the gods and the *apsaras*. Once again, Indra escorted him to the portal of Heaven where his special chariot stood by to carry the sage back.

After the sage had left, Indra went over to Airavata, his faithful and powerful elephant who stood at the gate. 'How majestic Airavata would look with the garland around his neck!' thought Indra. And not realizing how much this act would anger Durvasa, Indra placed the garland around Airavata's neck.

Airavata was thrilled to be wearing such an unusual garland. Indra commented on how majestic his *vahana* looked and patted him appreciatively before heading back to his palace.

Within minutes, however, a swarm of bees descended on the garland, attracted by its heady and irresistible fragrance. When Airavata could stand them no more, he ripped the garland away from his neck to prevent the bees from tormenting him.

The news of this incident somehow reached Durvasa. He was furious! The sage felt that he had been insulted and humiliated, for he had been given a distorted version of the story. Durvasa thought that Indra had treated his gift—which was as sacred as the *prasad,* or holy offerings, in his view—with disdain. Indra had not appreciated it enough and that was why he had given it away to his elephant, who had in turn torn it to pieces before throwing it away.

The sage shouted up to the gods in Heaven: 'You vain, disrespectful gods! You have become too proud because of eternal youthfulness and your power of

immortality! Well, let me put an end to that. From now on you will grow old like the mortals, and you will die too!'

Then he addressed Airavata specifically saying, 'Airavata, Elephant of the Clouds, you are far too vain and proud of your beauty for your own good. You need to be taught a lesson as well. From now, you will lose this beauty that you are so proud of and look just like any ordinary elephant.'

And almost immediately, Airavata lost his splendid milk-white countenance.

CHAPTER FIVE

THE CHURNING AND ITS JEWELS

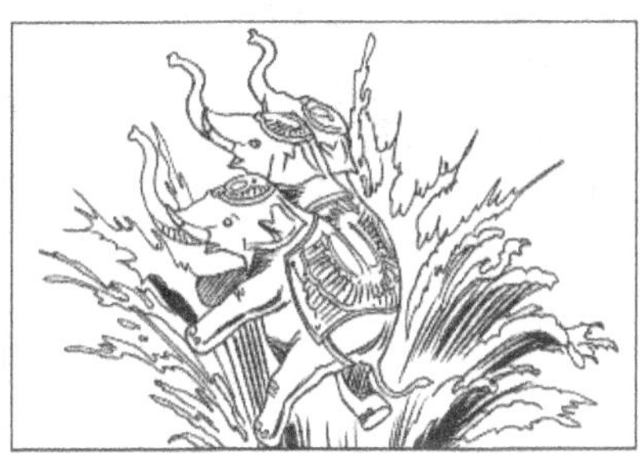

Airavata felt deeply saddened and embarrassed to be the cause of Durvasa's terrible curse. He was also upset at having lost his glowing whiteness. He knew he had been the reason for this horrible mess. If he had not thrown the garland away after being plagued by the bees, all of this wouldn't have happened.

He felt so guilty that he couldn't face Lord Indra or any of the other gods and so he went and hid himself in the Ocean of Milk, unwilling to appear before anyone.

'What have you done, O great sage!' cried several

hermits who happened to hear Durvasa's loud and public curse. 'Now you have made the universe unsafe. The *asuras* will soon be all-powerful and they will take advantage of your curse.'

The sage with the short temper soon realized that he had made a mistake. His curse would only endanger the universe, for once the gods grew old like the mortals, the powerful demons could vanquish them in no time. And if the demons became the rulers of the earth and Heaven, nothing would be safe any more, and evil would outdo goodness. The demons were arrogant, tyrannical and evil, and they did not believe in truth, goodness and righteousness.

Durvasa closed his eyes, and with immense concentration, he thought things over. He decided to make a few changes to his curse, as sages had the power to do that, even if they couldn't retract their curse once it was pronounced.

Now he proclaimed: 'The gods will once again regain their immortality and triumph over the law of ageing if they drink the *amrita*, or the nectar of immortality, that emerges from Kshirasagara, or the universal Ocean of Milk. The elixir shall emerge when the Ocean is churned and all will be well again.'

Lord Vishnu, the Preserver of the Universe, knew that it would be a struggle for the gods to acquire the coveted *amrita*, for it was hidden very deep in the Ocean of Milk and no one knew where it actually was. It was not possible for the gods to perform this task all by themselves. So the gods made overtures of friendship to the *asuras*, promising them a share of the *amrita* in return for their help. The celestial beings then went about requesting the huge Mount Mandara to be their churning staff, and the serpent king Vasuki to coil himself around the mountain so that he could be used as the churning rope.

As soon as the gods and the *asuras* began churning, standing on opposite sides of the mountain, the mountain began sinking into the ocean. Upon seeing the gods despair, Vishnu came to the rescue once again. He incarnated as Kurma, or the tortoise, and took on the entire weight of the mountain on his carapace, and the churning continued with no further interruption.

Decades passed, and the gods and *asuras* continued churning. In time, various objects began emerging in the cloud of foam and the swirling creamy waters of the churned ocean. First was the deadly poison Halahala, the fumes of which left the gods and the *asuras* terribly weakened. Upon sensing danger, Lord Shiva came to their rescue, cupping the poison in his palm and swallowing it. His wife, Parvati, clasped him gently by the throat, preventing the poison from spreading any lower than his throat. This is how Shiva became known as Neelakantha, or the blue-throated one.

Fourteen precious objects or creatures called the *ratnas* emerged from the Ocean of Milk. Of these, there was Kaustabha, the most precious jewel in the world; Sharanga and Shankha—Vishnu's bow and conch respectively; Parijat the evergreen flowering tree; the goddess of wine—Varuni; the wish-granting bountiful cow called Kamadhenu; the wish-bestowing tree called Kalpavriskha; the seven-headed celestial steed called Uchchaishravas; Chandra the Moon; Lakshmi the Goddess of Wealth; and finally, Dhanvantari, or the Physician of the Gods with an urn carrying the *amrita*.

As all these divine creatures emerged from the frothy waters, Airavata, who had been hiding away in the very

depths of this ocean for a long, long time, also came out. He arose from the Ocean of Milk, cleansed of his curse, and looking as spotless and white as he had once been.

As soon as the *asuras* spotted the *amrita*, they snatched the vessel away. But true to their ways, they began quarrelling among themselves. As the gods despaired of ever getting a bit of the *amrita*, it was left to Lord Vishnu to resolve matters. He assumed the form of a beautiful *apsara* called Mohini, and the *asuras* were so enchanted by her that they let her take the vessel of *amrita* away. By the time they realized they had been fooled, the gods had already had their share. They were immortal once again, and they returned triumphantly to Heaven, led by Indra atop who else but Airavata, who was once again restored to his former magnificence, as well as his role as the vehicle of the Lord of Heaven.

CHAPTER SIX

REVENGE AND RETRIBUTION

As Indra's vehicle, Airavata carried the Lord of Heaven to many great battles against evil *asuras*. The great elephant-king was very swift and could make his way across Heaven and earth at top speed. He was also a loyal companion, who stood by Indra's side and fought with him against fierce demons.

One such battle was against Vritra, a terrible *asura* who stood for everything wicked, and plagued the gods and humans with his evil ways. Like other demons, Vritra could take on various forms. He often appeared

as either a dragon or a serpent and was also known as *ahi*, or snake. He symbolized drought, and sometimes incarnated as a dragon blocking the course of rivers.

Vritra was a son of Tvashta, the Divine Carpenter and Smith, and he was created after Tvashta's first son Vishwarupa had been killed by Indra. The grief-stricken father wanted nothing more than to avenge his son's death.

Tvashta decided to perform a sacrifice that would give him a second son who could slay Indra. The sacrifice was soon underway, with Tvashta himself conducting it. However, as fate would have it, he mispronounced the mantra and that was a disastrous error, one that would cost him very, very dearly. When it was time for the final incantations, Tvashta should have said, 'May this son of mine be the slayer of Indra', but instead he accidentally muttered, 'May Indra be the slayer of this son of mine.'

From the sacrificial fire rose a terrible *asura*. He was named Vritra, or the encloser. He immediately swelled in size to stand tall. He was as large as the largest mountain. His hair was the colour of burnished copper, he had a fierce moustache and thick beard, and his eyes blazed in fury like the midday sun. He was armed with a magical trident. His father then ordered him to go and slay Indra. Obedient to the command, the demon began to seek the slayer of his elder brother.

He laid his plans out carefully. He started to serve the *asura* king, Puloman, who ruled over a big kingdom and was believed to be a benevolent leader. Vritra earned admiration for his courage and his strategic skills as a general. In time, he fell in love with Puloman's daughter Sachi and wanted to marry her. But Sachi refused Vritra, as he was working for her father.

Disappointed by Sachi's rebuff, Vritra left the service of Puloman. He dedicated himself to propitiating Lord

Shiva, and practised the severest of austerities to please this temperamental god.

Impressed by his devotion, Shiva appeared before him and blessed him with the boon that he could not be killed by any ordinary weapon or any implement known at that time. This made him nearly immortal. Pleased by the boon he had been granted, Vritra set about assembling a great army and set out to win a kingdom for himself, one greater than Puloman's. Those *asuras* who joined his army and were willing to fight for him were attracted by his strength and fearsome image.

With his great skills as a general and his new-found invincibility, Vritra in no time acquired a kingdom for himself. He also assumed a dragon-like form and used his powers to block the rivers from flowing in Heaven and on earth.

Soon everything began to wither and die. Plants wilted, trees shrivelled, animals went crazy with thirst, and people grew more and more desperate, praying to all the gods for a spot of rain.

Soon, the gods too felt threatened by the *asuras*, though they had defeated them a short while back during the *samudra manthan*, or churning of the Ocean of Milk. Seeing the rise in Vritra's power, they knew that the peace that had been won was short-lived.

Despite their requests and the pleading of the people on earth, Vritra kept the waters of the universe captive. He taunted the gods, jeering at their inability to subdue him. His ultimate aim was to become the King of Heaven, to win for himself Lord Indra's great wealth, especially his wonderfully white and magical elephant—Airavata.

The gods, frightened by his evil might, rushed to Lord Vishnu. They believed that Vishnu, being the Preserver of the Universe, would surely have a solution. They were led by Indra on his faithful Airavata, who covered the distance from Heaven to Vaikuntha, where Vishnu resided, in no time.

Lord Vishnu heard them out patiently, consoled them, and then reminded them of the boon Vritra had been granted by Shiva. If he had to die, his death could only be brought about by an extraordinary weapon.

Vishnu also revealed that Vritra would never be destroyed by ordinary means as the demon could not be killed with anything made of metal, wood, or stone, or anything that was dry or wet. He could also not be killed during the day or at night. Last but not least, whoever killed him could neither be standing nor flying.

Vishnu told the assembly of gods that the weapon that would destroy the *asura* would have to be fashioned out of the bones of a sage. This threw the gods into a tizzy as no weapon of such great power had ever been created in any of the three worlds of Heaven, earth and the underworld.

CHAPTER SEVEN

A SAGE'S AMAZING SACRIFICE

Lord Vishnu, with his all-seeing eyes and his ability to know the future, helped the gods devise a plan. He asked them to seek the help of the great, and deeply venerated sage, Dadhichi.

The gods knew that the *asuras* would never dare to approach the hermitage of Dadhichi, for the sage had extraordinary powers that would make them fear for their life. The gods, encouraged by Lord Vishnu, willingly entrusted all their weapons to Dadhichi for safekeeping.

When news spread that the gods had sought Dadhichi's help, the sage's wife, Lopamudra, was not at all pleased.

She said to her husband, 'An ascetic should never take sides in a war, especially in the kind that is being waged between the gods and the *asuras*. The battle between good and evil is an eternal one, and do you think that even an immensely powerful sage like you can influence this battle? Or take sides in this war without resolution? Now

that the gods' weapons are in your keeping, the *asuras* will think that you are their enemy and try to harm you. And the gods never mentioned how long you are to take care of their weapons. If something should happen to these weapons in our house, we will be blamed. Besides, we lead austere lives and have given up all worldly possessions and attachments. Dear husband, you were wrong to have taken on this terrible responsibility.'

The sage understood what his wife was trying to say, but he explained his position to her: 'I have given the gods my word. It is important to stand by the promise one makes. What is fated will happen, and no one can prevent it.'

Years and decades passed, and Dadhichi noted with alarm that the lustre of the divine weapons was beginning to diminish. Their might was slowly fading. The sage then used his power to dissolve all the weapons in water, after which he drank the very same water, thereby lodging all their powers in his bones.

As Vritra grew ever more strong, the gods realized that the hour of battle was drawing near. They went together to Dadhichi's hermitage to ask him to return their weapons. The trouble sage explained, 'I have bad news for you. Your weapons are no longer in the shape you gave them to me. Their power now resides in my bones. If I give up my life, you can have weapons made from my bones. And why shouldn't I make this sacrifice? After all, it will be for a worthy cause.'

The gods turned to Indra, their king. It was a tough decision. Indra was, of course, not at all keen on bringing death to the kind sage. However, he had no choice as the gods needed the weapons to battle Vritra. Dadhichi gave up his life without a qualm as it was for the greater good of the universe.

The bones of the great sage were then collected and handed over to Lord Vishwakarma, the Universal Architect, who forged a formidable weapon and called it the Vajra. This was the most powerful weapon ever made, and only Indra could wield it.

Lord Vishnu made space for the battle by taking three great strides that covered the entire universe. So the battle was fought in all spheres—on air, water and land.

A trio of gods—Varuna, the God of the Ocean, Soma, the Moon God and Agni, the God of Fire—was coaxed by Indra into assisting him in the fight against Vritra.

With the preparations all in place, Indra led the legion of gods to battle, riding on Airavata. The grand white elephant at the head of an army of immortal divine beings was a sight that would make any *asura* or *rakshasa* quiver in fear.

CHAPTER EIGHT

A MOST UNIQUE WEAPON

The two great armies met on the battlefield that had been created by Vishnu. Following the advice of the mighty Preserver of the Universe, Indra rode into battle on Airavata, for he could not kill Vritra if he stood on land or used his powers to fly.

At first, faced with a furious onslaught by the *asura* army, the gods were driven back, but they redoubled their efforts and slowly gained the advantage in battle. Soon they had the upper hand, and the demons' army gradually began to retreat.

Seeing his forces weakening, Vritra was enraged. He charged ahead and single-handedly stopped the advance of the army of gods. He let out a mighty roar, which caused many of the gods to faint. Heaven shook under his purposeful tread, which had the power to make everything shake and shudder.

It was then that Indra made his proposal.

He suggested said that instead of making the armies fight and causing such widespread destruction, only the two of them should battle. And whoever won the duel would take over the other's army.

Vritra laughed scornfully and agreed. He was much bigger than Indra, and was extremely confident because of the boon bestowed upon him by Lord Shiva. He had taken his victory for granted, even before the battle began.

Vritra hefted his mammoth mace and struck Airavata with it. However, Airavata was an old hand at combat techniques and he anticipated Vritra's move. The brave elephant rose in the air, in order to save his lord and master from the swinging mace. The mace missed Indra, but Airavata collapsed in pain.

However, Indra quickly gave Airavata some *amrita* to restore him. Airavata immediately revived, even stronger then before, and was also granted the gift of immortality.

The battle continued on an equal footing, and went on for many days and many nights. Years passed and neither of the two flagged in their efforts to emerge victorious. Vritra, being an *asura*, could change his form at will. He fought sometimes as a huge bird in the sky, sometimes as a snake, and at other times a fire-breathing dragon. However, Indra was also the God of War and his martial prowess was unmatched. Thus, he fought each of Vritra's monstrous forms without flagging. The loyal Airavata carried his Lord and manoeuvred around the difficult terrain across land, water and skies, matching Vritra's every move.

Indra and Vritra hurled taunts at each other. Vritra humiliated Indra for having slain his brother Vishwarupa in a cowardly manner. Provoked, Indra reached out and struck off Vritra's hand with his sword. In retaliation, and not in the least affected by the severed hand, Vritra swelled in size, bigger, bigger and bigger, until his mouth became as cavernous as a huge cave.

And in a trice, the demon swallowed both Lord Indra and his faithful mount, Airavata.

Despite being swallowed whole, Indra did not die, for he was protected by the grace of Vishnu, and Airavata in turn was protected by Indra. Thus they remained safe, but trapped inside Vritra.

Indra knew that the time had come for him to use the all-powerful Vajra that had been created out of the sage Dadhichi's bones, especially for this battle. Holding it aloft, and striking out with it, he sliced open the abdomen of the demon—and emerged triumphant, riding the great Airavata.

However, Vritra was also protected by his several

boons and he survived the onslaught of the Vajra as his stomach sealed up on its own. The battle continued, and Indra was, on occasion, forced to flee. He fought over and over with Vritra. In each battle, Indra finally emerged victorious because he was aided by powers granted to him by the divine trinity of Brahma, Vishnu and Shiva.

Vritra broke Indra's jaws during one battle, but was in turn thrown to the ground by Indra, who unleashed arrow after arrow upon him.

Then Indra destroyed all the ninety-nine fortresses of Vritra before he freed the rivers that had been captured by the demon.

One day, the two mighty warriors were battling by the sea. The sun was going down, and in the twilight, a huge wave washed up on the shore, spraying a great column of foam over the opponents.

Lord Vishnu had entered this foam to help Indra. The time had come for the prophecy to be fulfilled. The time of the day was perfect. It was neither day nor night, but a strange kind of twilight hour. The foam from the sea was not made of wood, stone, or metal; nor was it wholly wet or entirely dry. All the conditions seemed to comply with those of the prophecy.

Indra seized the foam and brought it crashing down on the demon, who immediately fell dead, for the foam was actually an extension of the all-mighty Lord

Vishnu. For this feat, Indra became known as Vritrahan, or 'slayer of Vritra'.

However, in the end, by having slain a creature that had emerged from a holy sacrifice, Indra knew he had committed a sin and needed to offer penance. So he retired to the banks of the holy lake at Manasarovar. Here, under extreme conditions, he meditated for a thousand years to expiate his wrongdoing. At long last, his sins forgiven, Indra stepped on to Airavata, who had waited by his side faithfully all those long years, and made his way back to Heaven.